P9-CRA-690

Text copyright © 2018 by Glen Huser
Illustrations copyright © 2018 by Milan Pavlović
Published in Canada and the USA in 2018 by Groundwood Books

Groundwood Books / House of Anansi Press
groundwoodbooks.com

We acknowledge for their financial support of our publishing program the
Canada Council for the Arts, the Ontario Arts Council and the Government
of Canada.

RECEIVED

MAY 1 4 2018

Library and Archives Canada Cataloguing in Publication
Huser, Glen, author
The snuggly / Glen Huser ; [illustrations by] Milan Pavlović.
Issued in print and electronic formats.
ISBN 978-1-55498-901-0 (hardcover). — ISBN 978-1-55498-902-7 (PDF)
I. Pavlović, Milan, illustrator II. Title.
PS8565.U823S68 2018
jC813'.54   C2017-905251-9   C2017-905252-7

The illustrations were done in color pencils and ink.
Design by Michael Solomon
Printed and bound in Malaysia

For Jakob, Gracie and Maeve — GH

To my parents, Branislav and Gordana — MP

THE SNUGGLY

GLEN HUSER

PICTURES BY
MILAN PAVLOVIĆ

 GROUNDWOOD BOOKS
HOUSE OF ANANSI PRESS
TORONTO   BERKELEY

THE DAY TODD's mama came home with a new baby, Todd's papa came home with something special too.

"What's that?" said Todd.

"It's a snuggly," said Papa. "It's for carrying little Ada so she'll be close and safe."

Papa showed Todd how it worked.

Sometimes Papa let Todd wear the snuggly too. But not with baby Ada in it. Todd put Banjo Bear inside instead.

"So he'll be close and safe," Todd said to Papa.

Todd was wearing the snuggly when it was time to go to school. He thought he would like to show it to everyone.

He went to ask Papa, but Papa was heading to work.

He went to ask Mama, but Mama was busy giving Ada a bath.

"They won't mind if I take the snuggly to school," he thought. "It's only for this morning."

On his way to meet Ivan at the end of the block, Todd found a treasure.

"I can paint this when I get home," he thought. "It will make a good rocket."

The treasure was too big for his
pocket, so Todd put it in the snuggly.
He moved Banjo Bear a bit so it
would fit.

"What is that you're wearing?" said Todd's friend Ivan.

"It's a snuggly," said Todd. "It keeps things close and safe."

"Good place for this," said Ivan. "Then I won't lose it."

"Okay, put it in," said Todd. He moved Banjo Bear and the rocket a bit so Ivan's book would fit.

As they went around a corner, Todd and Ivan ran into their friend Sara.

"That's a funny backpack!" Sara laughed.

"It's not a backpack," said Todd. "It's a front pack. A snuggly."

"Can I put this in?" said Sara. "Then I won't eat it right away."

"I think it will fit," sighed Todd. "But don't squash Banjo Bear."

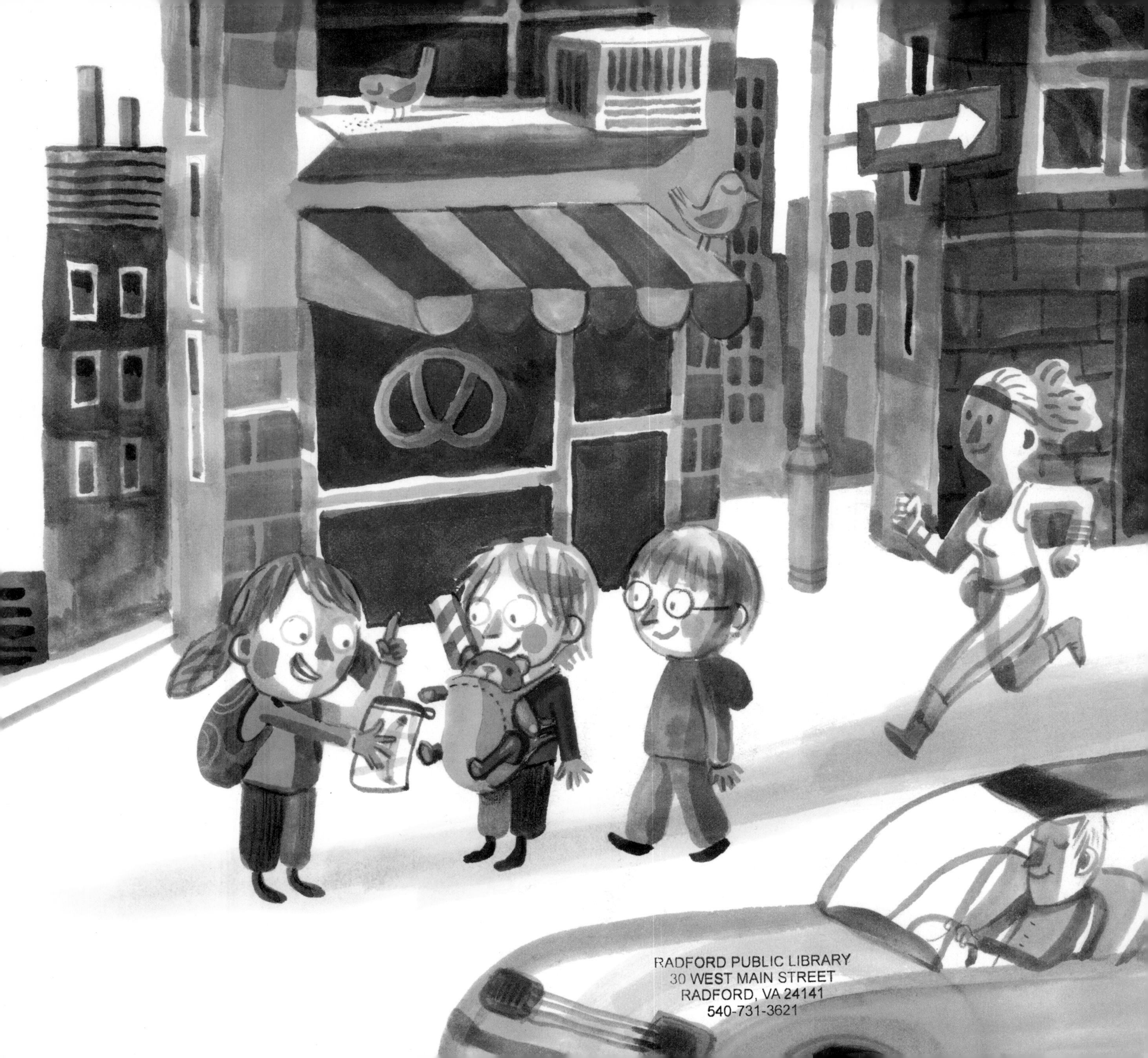

"Oh, look," said Ivan.

"Poor little thing," said Sara. "Is there room in your snuggly?"

"Maybe," said Todd. But he wasn't too sure. He moved Banjo Bear and the rocket and the library book and Sara's snack a bit and, yes, there was just enough room.

On the playground, Todd nearly tripped over his friend Anand.

Anand's eyes grew big when he saw what Todd was wearing.

"It's a snuggly," said Sara. "Keeps things safe."

"Neat," said Anand. "Good place for these."

"Yikes!" Todd shifted the straps of the snuggly. The kitten crawled over the jar and curled up beside Banjo Bear. One of Banjo Bear's arms popped out.

"Hey, look!" Sara laughed. "Miss Bale's done it again!"
"Surprise her," said Anand. "Put it in the snuggly."
"Then it won't get broken," said Ivan.

Before Todd could say anything, Anand pushed it in.
It made a scraping sound against the jar of pollywogs.
Banjo Bear's other arm popped out.

"Oh, my," said Miss Bale, as she came to get them to go into class. "I think you'd better go first for show and tell, Todd. Before you burst!"

But it was too late. As Todd went to the front of the class, the snuggly did burst. Everything spilled out.

Miss Bale's coffee mug clattered to the floor.

Anand's jar of pollywogs rolled down the aisle.

The lost kitten began racing around the room. "Hey, that's my cat!" A girl at the back of the class began chasing after the kitten.

Sara's snack fell on a boy's head.
Ivan's library book hit Miss Bale's toes.

The rocket flew into a jar of paint.
And Banjo Bear landed on his back on
the floor.

Everyone in the room laughed,
but Todd felt like crying.

"Never mind," said Miss Bale, and she gave Todd a big hug. "Only one strap has broken. I can fix it at recess time."

In a few minutes, everything had been picked up and the lost kitten was fast asleep in Banjo Bear's lap.

When it was time to go home for lunch, Miss Bale helped strap the snuggly onto Todd.

"There," she said. "Good as new, and, you know —"

"I know," Todd sighed. "A snuggly is good for just one thing. A baby … or a teddy bear."

Miss Bale tucked Banjo Bear into the snuggly.

Todd knew he would be safe and close all the way home.